PEEPING BEAUTY

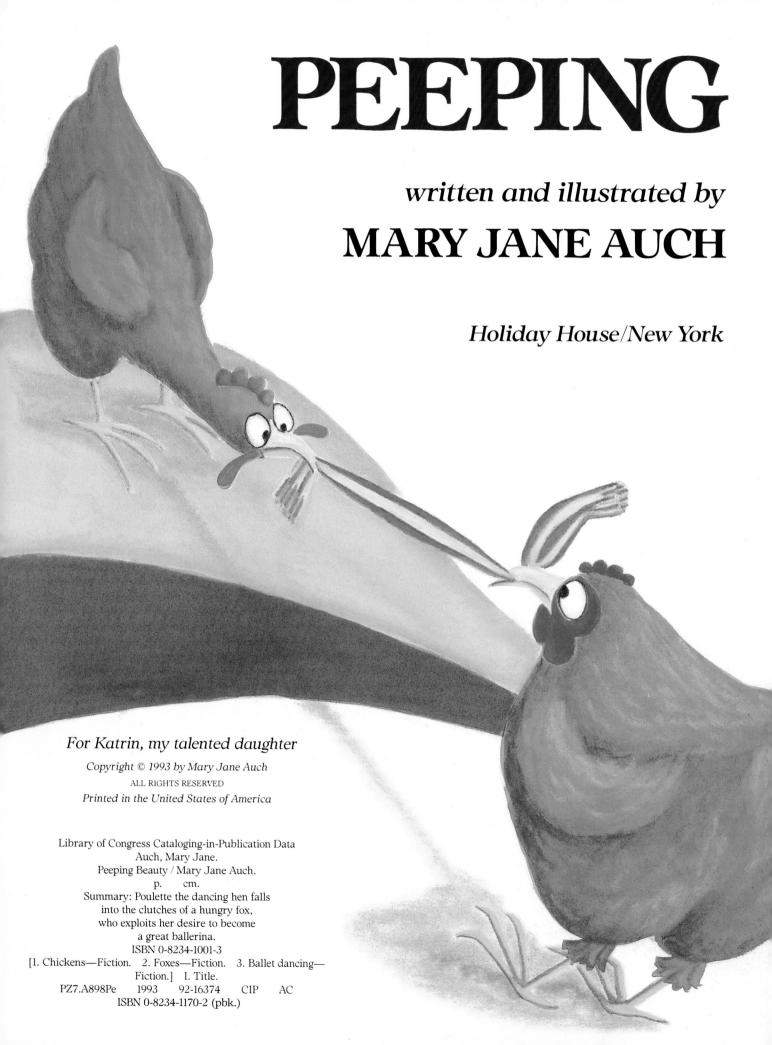

PEEPING

written and illustrated by

MARY JANE AUCH

Holiday House/New York

For Katrin, my talented daughter

Copyright © 1993 by Mary Jane Auch
ALL RIGHTS RESERVED
Printed in the United States of America

Library of Congress Cataloging-in-Publication Data
Auch, Mary Jane.
Peeping Beauty / Mary Jane Auch.
p.   cm.
Summary: Poulette the dancing hen falls
into the clutches of a hungry fox,
who exploits her desire to become
a great ballerina.
ISBN 0-8234-1001-3
[1. Chickens—Fiction.   2. Foxes—Fiction.   3. Ballet dancing—
Fiction.]   I. Title.
PZ7.A898Pe   1993   92-16374   CIP   AC
ISBN 0-8234-1170-2 (pbk.)

BEAUTY

Poulette wanted to be a famous ballerina. Every morning, while Gertrude and Philomena gossiped, Poulette did warm-up stretches and dreamed of stardom.

In the afternoon, while Claudine and Zelda scratched in the garden, Poulette danced her heart out.

"You're nuts," said Claudine. "Who ever heard of a dancing hen?"

"I'll be the first," said Poulette. "I have to follow my dream."

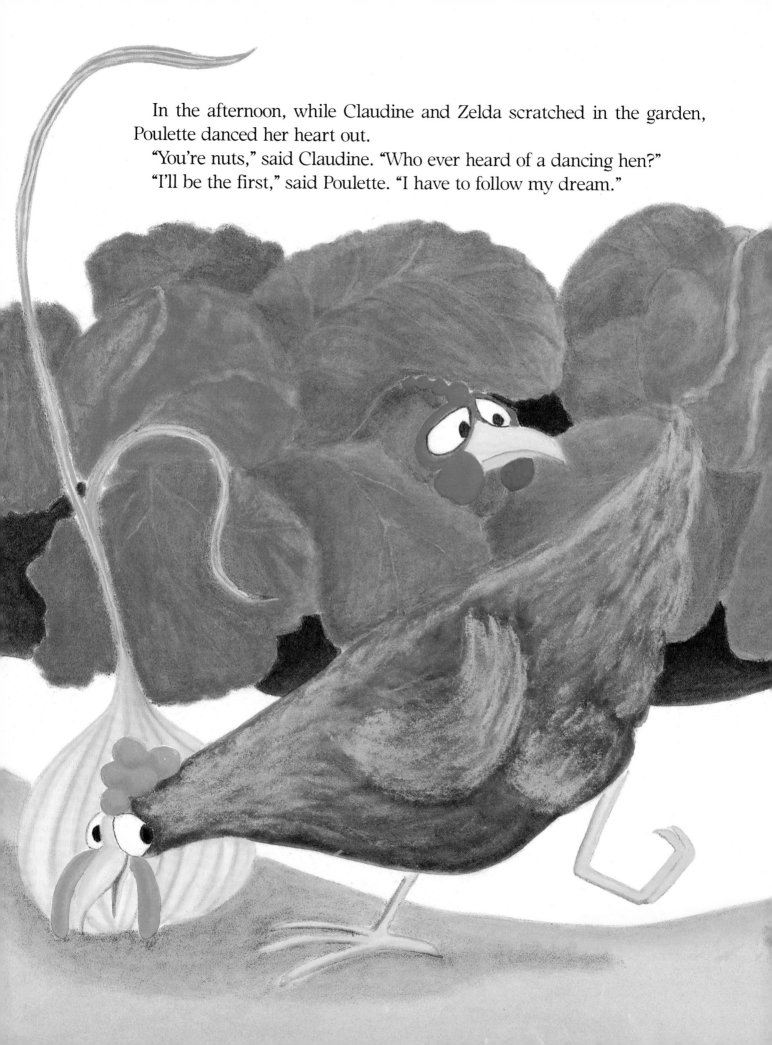

One day a fox appeared. "I've been watching you from my hill," he said to Poulette. "You have talent. Have you ever performed onstage?"

Poulette shook her head. "I've only danced around the farm. But I plan to be famous someday."

"I can help you!" the fox exclaimed. "I happen to be a talent scout in New York City. Right now, I'm hiring dancers for a new ballet called *Peeping Beauty*. Come audition for me tomorrow night."

"We hens never go off with strangers," said Poulette. "Especially strange foxes."

But a few days later, the fox was back. "I have everything ready," he said. "I've even built a special stage for you on my hill."

Poulette thought about her future. "I'd love to dance on a real stage," she said, "but you're a fox. How do I know you really want to help me?"

"Follow me," said the fox. "I have another surprise for you." He whipped something out from behind a rosebush. "I brought this tutu from New York especially for you. Isn't it stunning?"

"It's beautiful," Poulette said. "I'd love to dance in it . . . but I'll have to think about it."

The fox disappeared and came back a few hours later with a poster. "I've put these up all over town. Everyone wants to see you perform tonight. You can dance for a real audience."

"You'll be on a poster one minute and on a platter the next," clucked Claudine.

"Picture it," said the fox. "Hundreds of people will watch you dance. And when you take your bows, the audience will rise to its feet and applaud."

"Applaud for me?" asked Poulette. "Do you really think they will? Oh, I can't wait!"

"And after your performance, we'll have a lovely dinner," called the fox as he dashed up the hill. "Just the two of us."

"But only one of you will be eating," Zelda warned. "And it won't be you, Poulette."

"Stop trying to spoil my big chance!" snapped Poulette. "The fox wouldn't go to all this trouble just to eat me. You silly hens can spend your lives laying eggs and scratching for bugs, but I have talent. Tonight I'll become a star!"

When Poulette reached the stage that night, she was greeted by the fox.

"Why are you dressed like that?" she asked.

"You need a partner. I'll be the prince."

"Did lots of people come to see me dance?" Poulette peeked through the curtain, but she was blinded by the bright lights.

"There's not an empty seat out there. The whole audience is waiting for you to begin." The fox put on the music.

As the first notes floated over the stage, Poulette was no longer an ordinary hen. She became the lovely young princess, Peeping Beauty, and danced the best performance of her life.

"It's time for Peeping Beauty to fall asleep now," said the fox in a stage whisper. "Then I'll kiss you awake and we'll dance the finale."

Poulette pretended to prick her wing on the spindle. After a series of dizzying turns, she swooned onto a couch in center stage.

She waited for the fox's kiss, but nothing happened. When she opened her eyes, the fox's lips weren't puckered up at all. His sharp teeth glinted in the spotlight.

Poulette started to get up. "The finale!" she gasped.

"This *is* the finale," he said. "It's also the dinner, and you're the main course."

"You can't eat me in front of an entire audience," shrieked Poulette.
"There *is* no audience," said the fox.
"Then surely you couldn't eat a hen as talented as me."
"A chicken dinner is still a chicken dinner, no matter how talented she is,"
said the fox.

Suddenly Poulette had an idea. "All those hours of practice have made my muscles strong and hard . . . and tough. They don't call me 'thunder drumsticks' for nothing!" she shouted.

In one quick, graceful move, Poulette leaped up and did a *tour jeté*, knocking over the fox. "You're not having me for dinner, buddy. Your hen-eating days are over!"

The fox struggled to his feet, but Poulette was too fast for him. Before he knew what was happening, she toppled him with a *grand jeté*. He rolled over the edge of the hill. Poulette chased him all the way to the bottom.

The fox tumbled to a stop against the chicken coop. The other hens came running.

"All this exercise has made me hungry," said Poulette. "I think we should have fox for dinner."

"That's ridiculous," said the fox. "Chickens don't eat foxes."

"Who says?" asked Gertrude. "There's no law against it. Let's have fox chops with applesauce."

"Or maybe roast fox with chestnut stuffing," suggested Philomena.

"Let's have a picnic," said Zelda. "We'll grill foxburgers."

The fox tried to get up, but the hens jumped on top of him. "How can you say these things?" he cried. "I'm not a meal. I'm a fox . . . with feelings!"

"What am *I*, chopped chicken liver?" yelled Poulette. "You didn't think about *my* feelings when I was going to be *your* dinner."

"That's different," said the fox.

"I see," said Poulette. "Zelda, go get our roasting pan. Gertrude, you start the fire."

"No!" howled the fox. "Please let me go. I'll do anything."

"You promise you'll never eat another hen?" asked Poulette.

"No hens, I promise! No roosters, no ducks, no turkeys, no geese! I'll become a vegetarian!"

The hens laughed as they let the fox escape.
"Do you think he'll keep his word?" asked Gertrude.
"Probably not," said Poulette. "A fox is still a fox, no matter what he promises. But a talented hen will never be a chicken dinner."